An I Can Read Book™

Minnie and Moo

AND THE POTATO FROM PLANET X

by
**Den s
Cazet**

HarperCollins*Publishers*

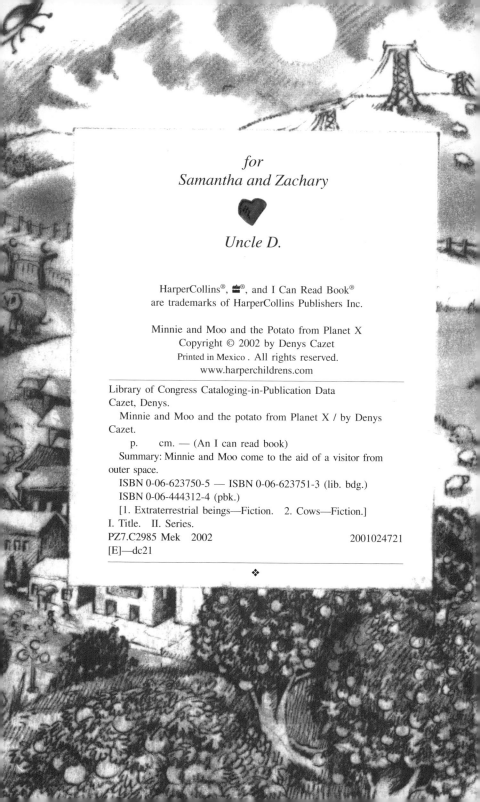

for
Samantha and Zachary

Uncle D.

HarperCollins®, 🔖®, and I Can Read Book®
are trademarks of HarperCollins Publishers Inc.

Minnie and Moo and the Potato from Planet X
Copyright © 2002 by Denys Cazet
Printed in Mexico . All rights reserved.
www.harperchildrens.com

Library of Congress Cataloging-in-Publication Data
Cazet, Denys.
  Minnie and Moo and the potato from Planet X / by Denys
Cazet.
      p.   cm. — (An I can read book)
  Summary: Minnie and Moo come to the aid of a visitor from
outer space.
    ISBN 0-06-623750-5 — ISBN 0-06-623751-3 (lib. bdg.)
    ISBN 0-06-444312-4 (pbk.)
    [1. Extraterrestrial beings—Fiction.   2. Cows—Fiction.]
I. Title.   II. Series.
PZ7.C2985 Mek   2002   2001024721
[E]—dc21

❖

A Summer Day

Minnie and Moo lay in the tall grass.

The sun was bright and hot.

"I love summer," said Moo.

"Mmm," said Minnie.

She raised her chin to the sun.

She rubbed on some lotion.

"What's that?" asked Moo.

5

"Sunscreen," said Minnie.

"I'm getting a little red."

"Not that," said Moo. "That!"

Minnie felt her chin. "This?"

"Up there," said Moo. "In the sky."

"Moo, what are you talking about?"

"LOOK!" said Moo.

Something sputtered

across the treetops.

It bounced into the hay field.

It plowed across the pasture

toward Minnie and Moo.

Closer and closer it came,

and then it stopped.

Moo looked at Minnie.

"Must be the new tractor," she said.

The Salesman

Minnie waved the dust away.

"It doesn't look like a tractor,"
she said. "It has fins."

"The farmer must have ordered
the newest model," said Moo.

A door slid open.

A creature with one eye stepped out.

"See," said Moo.

"There's the tractor salesman."

"Moo," whispered Minnie,

"how many salesmen

have green hair,

wires in their ears,

and bumpy red skin?"

"There's that kid who works
in the coffee shop," said Moo.

"Moo! This is a potato
with one eye!"

"Shhh," said Moo. "Here he comes."

11

The potato with one eye bowed.

"Greetings, O great, round earthlings.

May I know your names?"

"I am Minnie," said Minnie,

"and this is my best friend, Moo."

"I am pleased to meet with you,

Minnie and My Best Friend, Moo.

My name is Spud.

I am from the planet X.

I make deliveries

for Universal Package Service.

As your double eyeballs can see,

my UPS space truck has crashed.

I must have another ship

and five gallons of space fuel.

You must help me.

We must go fast."

The spaceman looked at his watch.
"We only have thirty minutes
to stop the Big Bump!"

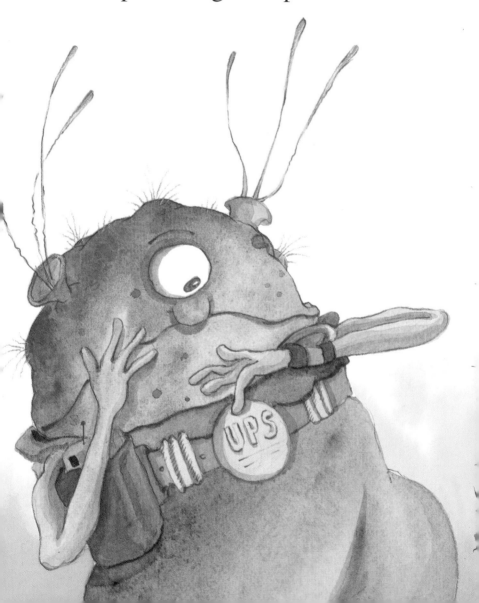

The Big Bump

Moo stared at the spaceman.

"The Big Bump?" she asked.

"The Big Bump," said the spaceman.

He held up a small package.

"This is a tube of Anti-Bump Cream.

It is used to prevent the planets

from bumping into each other."

"Without it," Spud said, "the earth
and all the other planets
will bump themselves to bits."
Moo looked at the package.
"This says:
'RUSH!—*Same Day Service.*'"

"I know," Spud said. "It is my fault.

I stopped for donuts."

"We only have thirty minutes

before the Big Bump and you stopped

for donuts!" said Minnie.

"It wasn't *all* my fault," said Spud.

"Traffic was bad.

I took a wrong turn at Mars.

I ran out of space fuel."

"This is serious," said Moo.

"Serious," said the spaceman.

"I could lose my job over this!"

The Space Tractor

Minnie looked at the space truck.

"Can't you fix it?" she asked.

"No," said Spud.

"I need another spaceship—now!"

Moo pointed down the hill.

"The farmer's tractor!" she said.

"We drove it to the moon."

"And back," added Minnie.

"Perfect," said the spaceman,

grabbing a tool kit.

"I can use parts from my old ship."

Minnie, Moo, and Spud

ran to the tractor.

"I must make a few changes,"
said Spud. "Hand me my blowtorch."
Some of the farm animals
wandered over to watch
the work on the tractor.
"Is it broken?" asked Bea Holstein.
"No," said Moo. "We're making
a few changes for space travel."

"Oh," said Bea.

Bea looked at the spaceman.

She whispered to her sister, Madge,

"That must be the new

tractor salesman."

"Not much to look at, is he?"

said Madge.

"Twenty minutes!" said the spaceman.

Space Fuel

The spaceman jumped off the tractor.

"There!" he said. "Now all we need

is five gallons of space fuel."

Moo took off the gas cap.

She looked inside.

"Plenty of gas," she said.

"Gas?" said the spaceman. "Gas?"

"Yes," said Moo. "It's almost full."

Spud looked into the tank.

"Oh, no!" he said. "Gas!

Gas is not space fuel!

I must remove this gas!

I must have five gallons

of space fuel! Hurry!"

All the animals looked at Moo.

"Moo," said Minnie,

"think of something."

"And hurry up!" said the rooster.

"I have friends coming for lunch."

The spaceman looked at his watch.

"Fifteen minutes," he said.

Moo Thinks

Moo paced back and forth.

"Space fuel," she muttered.

"Where do we get space fuel?"

The spaceman pointed

at Bea and Madge Holstein.

"Right there," he said.

"Hey!" said Bea. "I didn't touch it!"

"Me either," said Madge.

Moo froze.

"Wait a minute!" she said.

Minnie pushed the crowd back.

"Please, stand back," she said.

"Moo is having a thought."

Moo looked at the spaceman.

"What color is space fuel?" she asked.

"White," said Spud.

"And does space fuel taste good
with chocolate-chip cookies?"

"Yes, yes," Spud said. "It's space fuel!"

"MILK!" cried Moo.

"MILK is space fuel!"

"Not just *any* milk," warned Spud.

"It must have a very, very, very

high fat content."

Everyone looked at Minnie.

"What?" she asked.

"Minnie," said Moo, "you have
the highest fat content in the county."

"So?" said Minnie.

Moo handed Minnie a clean bucket.

"Five gallons, please."

"But Moo, I—"

"Ten minutes," said the spaceman.

Minnie Gives Her All

Everyone waited.

Everyone stared.

"Moo," whispered Minnie.

"I need the electric milker."

"Broken," said Moo.

"I need the farmer—"

"Gone to town," said Moo.

33

"Five minutes!" said Spud.

"I'm too nervous," cried Minnie.

"Everyone is staring at me!"

"Everyone out of the barn,"

Moo ordered.

34

"But Moo," said Minnie.

"The farmer always sings to us."

"We can sing to you," said Moo.

"How about your favorite song?"

Minnie nodded.

Moo hurried out of the barn.

"All right, everyone," she said,

tapping on a rusty pipe.

"Ready . . . one, two, three!"

"Home, home on the range,

Where the deer and the—"

"A little lower," shouted Minnie.

"More like the farmer."

"Once more," said Moo.

"Ready . . . one, two, three!"

"Home, home on the range,

Where the deer and the antelope play,

Where seldom is heard—"

"That's it!" cried Minnie.

"Five gallons of space fuel!"

Everyone rushed back into the barn.

"One minute!" warned the spaceman.

Minnie and Moo poured the warm milk

into the farmer's tractor.

"Stand back!" the spaceman yelled.

He pushed a red button.

The tractor roared into the sky.

"I hope he doesn't stop for donuts," said Moo.

"I hope he doesn't need any more space fuel," moaned Minnie.

Sunrise

Minnie and Moo

lay under the old oak tree.

"Are we still here?" Moo asked.

"I don't know," said Minnie.

"I'm afraid to open my eyes."

"I hear birds," said Moo.

She opened one eye.

43

"I see the old oak tree."

Minnie opened her eyes.

"I see the summer sky."

"He made it!" said Moo.

"The broken space truck is gone,"
said Minnie. "And there's
the tractor!"

Minnie picked up a pink box.

"What's this?"

"There's a note on it," said Moo.

Moo read the note out loud:

Dear Minnie

and My Best Friend, Moo—

I returned early this morning

to clean up my mess.

You were asleep.

I did not wish to wake you.

I hope the farmer likes the new things

I have added to his tractor.

He will be able to go much faster

when he presses the red button.

> *Thank you for your help.*
>
> *Love,*
>
> *Spud*

Moo opened the box.

"Oh my," she said. "Donuts!"

"Yum," said Minnie.

"Any cream puffs?"